Praise for
SOPHIE KINSELLA

"A Sophie Kinsella novel is like
a box of Valentine's Day chocolates."
—*USA Today*

"Kinsella has a genuine gift for comic writing."
—*The Boston Globe*

Praise for the
Fairy Mom and Me
series

"Inventive and charming while staying
grounded in realistic, everyday situations, to which
readers should have an easy time relating. Definitely
deserving of a place on the nightstand."
—*Booklist*

"Messages about the virtues of patience and not taking
shortcuts are handled with a light touch—most readers
will be content to laugh over the fairy magic hijinks."
—*Publishers Weekly*

"Goofy humor and surprising emotional depth
make this early chapter book appealing. . . . Plenty
of dialogue, direct storytelling, and easy sentence
structure lend the book to transitional reading, but
the episodic chapters can also serve as readalouds."
—*The Bulletin*

SOPHIE KINSELLA

Fairy Unicorn Wishes

illustrated by
Marta Kissi

A Yearling Book

This is a work of fiction. Names, characters, places, and incidents either are the product of the author's imagination or are used fictitiously. Any resemblance to actual persons, living or dead, events, or locales is entirely coincidental.

Text copyright © 2020 by Sophie Kinsella
Cover art and interior illustrations copyright © 2020 by Marta Kissi

All rights reserved. Published in the United States by Yearling, an imprint of Random House Children's Books, a division of Penguin Random House LLC, New York. Originally published in hardcover in the United States by Delacorte Press, an imprint of Random House Children's Books, New York, in 2020.

Yearling and the jumping horse design are registered trademarks of Penguin Random House LLC.

Visit us on the Web! rhcbooks.com
Educators and librarians, for a variety of teaching tools, visit us at RHTeachersLibrarians.com

Library of Congress Cataloging-in-Publication Data is available upon request.

ISBN 978-0-593-12051-4 (pbk.)

Printed in the United States of America
10 9 8 7 6 5 4 3 2 1
First Yearling Edition 2020

For Diggory

Contents

Meet Fairy Mom and Me

Hi there. My name is Ella Brook and I live in a town called Cherrywood with my mom, my dad and my baby brother, Ollie.

My mom looks normal, just like any other mom . . . but she's not. Because she can turn into a fairy. All she has to do is stamp her feet three times, clap her hands, wiggle her bottom and say, "Marshmallow,"... and POOF! She's Fairy Mom. Then if she says, "Toffee apple," she's just Mom again.

All the girls in my family turn into fairies when they grow up. My Aunty Jo and Granny did. They can all fly and become invisible and do real magic. Mom and Aunty Jo also have a really cool wand called a Computawand V5. It has magic powers, a computer screen, Fairy Apps, Fairy Mail and Fairy Games!

The problem is that Mom is still not very good at doing magic spells, even though

she works really hard at her lessons on FairyTube with her Fairy Teacher, Fenella. But one day she's going to get everything right.

When I'm grown up, I'll be a fairy like her! Mom calls me her Fairy in Waiting. I'll have big sparkly wings and my own beautiful shiny crown, and I'll be able to do magic just like Mom. I already know what my first spell will be. I'll wish for a unicorn of my very own. Although I can't do spells yet, I can play with my magic wardrobe. You'll meet Wardrobe later.

Being a Fairy in Waiting is a big secret. I'm not allowed to tell anyone, not even my best friends, Tom and Lenka. And I definitely can't tell my Not-Best Friend, Zoe. She is the meanest girl ever and she lives next door. Sometimes I think she might find out about Mom being a fairy.

But she hasn't yet. And life in a fairy family is fun! Even when there's a hitch or a glitch . . .

Fairy Spell #1

UPERIDOO!

The Day We Flew to School

It was time for school and we were going to be late. I knew this because Mom was running around the house shouting, "Where's my bag? Where's my bag?"

"I'll find it," Dad said. He looked under the table and in the fridge. "Not here. Where did you see it last?"

"I don't know!" Mom wailed. She threw all the sofa cushions on the floor, but her bag wasn't on the sofa. It wasn't in the microwave either.

I quickly looked in all the drawers. Ollie thought we were playing a game. He pointed at the ceiling and said, "Weezi-weezi-weezi!"

"All right," Mom said. "There's nothing for it." She stamped her feet three times, clapped her hands, wiggled her bottom and said, "Marshmallow," . . . and POOF! She was a fairy. Then she picked up her Computawand from the table. Most of the time it looks just like a normal phone, but as soon as

she touches it, the screen starts
to glow and it grows into a wand. Mom says
a wand needs a fairy's touch to come alive.

Fairy Mom waved her Computawand,
pressed a code on the screen—*bleep-bleep-bloop*—and said, "Bageridoo!"

Nothing happened.

I looked at Dad, and Dad looked at me.

Mom says when she was at school she was
so busy doing math and playing tennis that
she didn't have time to practice her spells.
Granny says if only she used an old-fashioned
wand instead of that silly Computawand, then
her spells would work *much* better.

"I don't think the spell worked," I said anxiously. "Should we just keep looking for the bag?"

"Well, it *should* have worked," Mom said. She pressed her Computawand again. "What's wrong with this thing?"

"Look," Dad said. He pointed through the open window. "What's that?"

We all peered out. There was a sort of multicolored cloud in the sky. It was getting bigger and bigger.

"What *is* that?" Mom asked.

"It's coming toward us," Dad said.

"Bags!" I said. "Lots of bags! It looks like it's going to rain bags."

The cloud was right above us. It rustled and quivered. There was a tremble of thunder.

Then suddenly we heard a loud bang and the bags started raining down all over the house and the yard. There were all sorts of bags. There were handbags, carrier bags and paper bags. There was a unicorn backpack and a pink bag with a big black buckle.

"Ooh," Mom said.

"I like that one!"

I loved the unicorn backpack best. It was all glittery.

Some of the bags landed in the yard, but some came down the chimney and some fluttered in through the window. One brown paper bag blew itself up with air, started dancing in the fruit bowl, did a waltz with a banana, then popped.

A beach bag landed on Dad's head. "Get off!" he said.

"Oops," Mom said. "I don't know how *that* happened. I'm sure I said the right spell." She started bashing her Computawand again.

"Is this your bag?" Dad asked. He was holding up a black handbag.

"Oh, *there* it is!" Mom said. "Thank you! Where was it?"

"On the door handle," Dad said. "Where it always is. And isn't it time for you to leave for school? Come on, Ollie. Let's clear up the mess."

"Toffee apple!" Fairy Mom said.

And then she was just Mom again.

I was getting worried because today was a special Be on Time Day. Everyone who came to school on time would get a sticker from our teacher, Miss Amy. The pupil who arrived first would get a special shiny sticker.

I really, really wanted a shiny sticker. But it was already eight o'clock. School starts at half past eight, so we needed to get going.

"Quick, Mom!" I said.

I ran out the door, lugging my school bag. Next door, my Not-Best Friend Zoe and her mom were coming out of their house. Zoe usually leaves earlier than us because she does swimming or ice skating before school. She is a very busy girl.

I've known Zoe all my life, since we were both babies in strollers. Her mom always says, "Ella and Zoe are best friends! They love each other!"

But she doesn't know how mean Zoe is to me. Zoe pinches me when no one's looking.

She says nasty things when Miss Amy isn't around. And once she ripped my brand-new furry pencil case. On purpose.

"Morning, Ella!" Zoe's mom said before she got into her car.

Zoe turned around so her mom couldn't see her, then stuck out her tongue. "You're going to be late!" she said. "We're going to beat you! Loser! Bye-ee!"

She laughed her horrible laugh, jumped into the car and slammed the door.

Their car started and roared off down the road.

"Mom!" I yelled. "Come on!"

I really, *really* didn't want Zoe to get the shiny sticker.

At last we got in our car and set off.

Mom said, "Don't worry, Ella—we'll be there in no time! I'll drive super fast."

But as we turned the corner, we saw a traffic jam. Not just a little traffic jam, but a GREAT BIG traffic jam. There were cars and buses and even a big truck, all squashed together in the road.

"Oh no," Mom said. "Well, I'm sure it will move soon."

But it didn't. We sat there and sat there and nothing moved. Some cars started to honk their horns. Other cars turned around to go a different way—but *we* couldn't go a different way. I was getting more and more worried.

"Don't worry," Mom said. "I'm sure Miss Amy won't mind if you're late."

"But I can't be late for school!" I wailed. "I *can't*! Today is Be on Time Day! If we get to school on time, we get a sticker!"

"A sticker?" Mom asked.

"Yes, a sticker! And whoever arrives first gets a special shiny sticker. And Zoe will get there first, and she'll get the shiny sticker and I won't."

"A shiny sticker . . ." Mom thought for a moment. "Well, that's different."

She stamped her feet three times, clapped

her hands, wiggled her bottom on the car seat and said, "Marshmallow,"... and POOF! She was a fairy.

Her shimmery wings were all squashed up in the car. I couldn't believe it. "Mom, someone will see you!"

"No one's looking," she said. "Now let's get out of this traffic jam."

"How are we going to do that?" I asked.

"We're going to fly," she said.

"Fly?" My eyes went wide. I had never flown in a car before.

"Of course! But first we need to be invisible."

Mom took her Computawand out of her bag. The screen started to glow and it grew into a wand. She pointed it at herself, at me and at the car, pressed a code on the screen—*bleep-bleep-bloop*—and said, "Inviseridoo!"

I felt a funny tingling. "Are we both invisible now?" I looked around. "Is the car invisible too?"

"Yes." Mom looked pleased. "The spell worked perfectly. Right, I just need to do the flying spell—"

BANG!

CRASH!

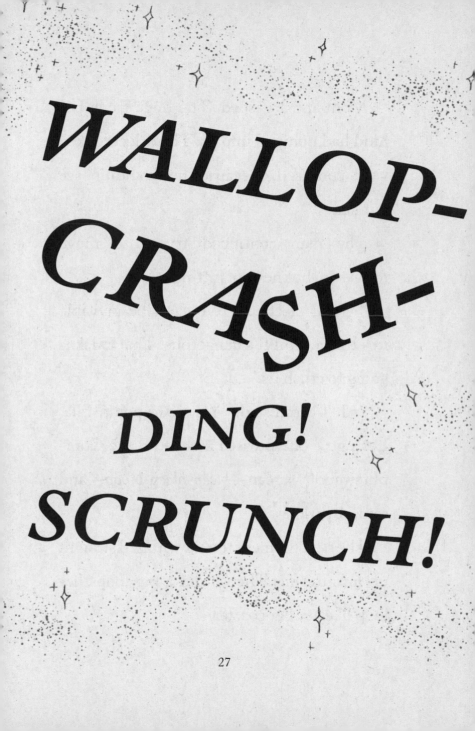

WALLOP-
CRASH-

DING!

SCRUNCH!

Mom and I gasped. The huge truck be-hind had bumped into us. The driver looked very confused, because he couldn't see our car.

The man continued trying to move forward—but he kept hitting us.

"Mom!" I cried. "We can't be invisible in a traffic jam! It's dangerous! That truck is going to crush us."

"Ah," Mom said. "Yes, good point, Ella. Let's go." She pressed a code on the Com-putawand screen—*bleep-bleep-bloop*—and said, "Uperidoo!"

The next moment the car whizzed straight up into the air. Then it did a big loop-the-loop like a roller coaster.

"This is amazing!" I shouted. "This is so cool!"

"Flyeridoo!" shouted Mom, and the car started flying along like a plane. I stared out the window at the streets below, and all the cars and buses and trucks in the traffic jam. Everything looked so small. The cars were just like toy cars, the people like tiny dolls.

Even my school looked like a toy school. There it was, ahead in the distance.

"Have you ever flown a car before, Mom?" I asked.

"No, but I've flown a carpet," she said. "And a car is *much* easier." She looked very pleased with herself.

A flock of birds came near, and Mom
quickly flew the car even higher so we didn't
bump into them. They couldn't see us, but
I waved and giggled.

"Look!" Mom said, pointing out the window. "We're nearly at school. Wasn't that
quick! We'd better head down. I'll try to land

behind that tree." She pressed another code on her Computawand—*bleep-bleep-bloop*. "Downeridoo!"

But the car didn't go down. It kept flying. It was flying and flying, away from my school, away from our town. Fairy Mom started bashing her Computawand.

I stared out the window. I couldn't believe it. My school was disappearing into the distance.

"No, car!" I said. "Go back! Back!"

"Downeridoo!" Fairy Mom shouted. "Downeridoo! Down, car! DOWNERIDOO!"

The car suddenly started to go down. It landed in a field. All we could see was grass and trees.

Mom and I looked at each other.

"Oops," Mom said. "I don't know how *that* happened. Maybe flying a car isn't so easy after all."

"Where are we?"

"Let me see. . . ." Mom looked at the navigation system and

bit her lip. "Oh no, we've gone FAR too far."

We got out of the car. There weren't any roads or people or houses. All we could see was a single cow.

"We'll be really late for school." My voice trembled, but I managed not to cry. "I won't get a shiny sticker, and Zoe will laugh at me."

"Zoe will *not* laugh at you," Mom said. She put her arms around me and gave me a big hug. She wasn't easy to hug, with her

wings still scrunched up from being in the car. "And we will *not* be late."

"But, Mom," I said, "look at the car!"

The car was all crumpled up from landing in the field. It had a big dent in the back where the truck had bashed it, and a wheel had fallen off.

"Oh no," Mom said. "That's not good. Your dad won't be pleased."

"How will we get to school now?" I asked. "What will we do?"

"We will—" Mom stopped and thought.

"What?"

"We will—"

"WHAT?"

"We will walk," Mom said. "With our magic legs."

"Magic legs?" I asked. "What are magic legs?"

"They are legs that can walk extra fast. I'll do another spell. I haven't done it before, but it can't be that difficult to make magic legs." Mom waved her Computawand and pressed a code on the screen—*bleep-bleep-bloop*. **"Legseridoo!"** she said.

Suddenly I had a strange feeling in my legs. It was a wibbly-wobbly feeling. I looked down and gasped. "Mom!" I said. "My legs have turned to jelly!"

They were all red and shiny. I looked at

Mom and she had jelly legs too, only hers were green.

I was wobbling everywhere, and so was Mom. Wibble-wobble-wibble-wobble.

"Oh no!" Mom said. "These are no good for walking!" She looked crossly at her Computawand. "I really don't understand what went wrong."

Then I heard a snorting sound. I looked around and saw something rushing toward us. That something was the cow we had seen earlier.

Only it wasn't a cow at all. It was a bull, with two sharp horns on its head. It was big and brown, and it looked angry.

When an angry bull is charging toward you, you really, really don't want jelly legs.

"Mom!" I yelled. "Watch out! We've got jelly legs and a bull is coming!"

"He can see us!" Mom gasped. "The Inviseridoo spell has worn off!"

She waved her Computawand and pressed a code—*bleep-bleep-bloop*. "Inviseridoo!" she shouted. "Quick!"

We were invisible again, but the bull was still charging toward us and we still had jelly legs.

"Yikes!" Mom said. "It can't see us, but it must be able to smell us." She jabbed her Computawand. "Legseridoo!"

"Help!" I cried. "It's getting close! Help! Do another spell, Mom."

"Maybe this one is better." Mom pressed a code on the screen—*bleep-bleep-bloop*—and shouted, "Come on, you stupid wand! Come on. . . . Rocketeridoo!"

And our legs weren't jelly anymore. Now we had rocket

blasters on our backs. Just as the bull reached us, we shot high up into the air. Mom grabbed my hand and I screamed. "Aargh!"

We did a loop-the-loop, around and around, and I shouted, "Wheeee!" and Mom laughed. It was very cold and very exciting and a little scary at the same time.

"You're a superhero!" Mom said. "You're Super-Ella!"

"And you're Super–Fairy Mom!" I laughed.

"And look—we're here!" Mom said.

She pointed below us, and I gasped. We had whooshed so fast that we were nearly at my school.

And then I spotted something else.

"Look, Mom! There's the traffic jam we were stuck in before. And that's what was causing it!"

Just around the corner from school, a tree had fallen across the road. Some people were trying to move it, but it was very heavy.

"Wait a moment," Mom said. "I can fix this."

Even though I wanted my shiny sticker, I wanted to help too. We dove down toward the tree and hovered in the air. I could tell that Mom was thinking. Then she pressed a code on her Computawand

screen—*bleep-bleep-bloop*. She waved it in a circle and shouted, "Whirleridoo!"

A whirlwind started to blow, around and around. It lifted the tree right up into the air.

"Ooh!" cried all the people watching. The tree rose higher and higher, then came safely down to rest in a nearby garden.

At once the traffic started moving again. All the people on the pavement cheered. One man cried, "It's a miracle!"

Mom looked pleased with herself. She patted her Computawand. "Maybe I should be a traffic cop," she said.

I smiled, shaking my head. Together,

Mom and I floated down into the school playground. I was glad to have normal legs again. We both had sticky-uppy hair from whooshing around in the sky, but luckily Mom had a hairbrush in her bag.

"All right," she said. "Let's go and get that sticker." She waved her wand, pressed a code—*bleep-bleep-bloop*—and said, "Stoperidoo!"

At once, we weren't invisible anymore. We didn't have rocket blasters anymore. Then Mom said, "Toffee apple,". . . and she wasn't Fairy Mom anymore. She was just Mom.

We walked into school and to my classroom. None of my classmates had arrived yet. My teacher, Miss Amy, looked up and gave me a big smile.

"Hello, Ella," she said. "You're the first to arrive today! You get the special shiny sticker!"

She gave me a sticker with pink sparkles, and I put it on my sweatshirt. I felt so, *so* happy.

"Everyone else has been stuck in a terrible

traffic jam!" Miss Amy said. "Didn't you get stuck too?"

Mom looked at me, and I looked at her.

"We did," Mom said. "But then we managed to get out. We were lucky." She winked at me. "I'd better tell Dad that he needs to take the car to the garage. It's *always* breaking down in the wrong place."

Mom kissed me and went off to work. I sat down at my desk and started doing some coloring. Then Zoe came dashing into the classroom. Her cheeks were pink and she ran in so fast she didn't see me.

"I'm first!" she said. "Everyone else is stuck in traffic, but we left the car and ran all the way! I'm first! I'm first, Miss Amy! I'm going to get the special shiny sticker!"

"Actually," Miss Amy said, "Ella was first."

Zoe went all quiet. She turned around and saw me. Her cheeks grew pinker. She looked at my sticker and her eyes went very big—then small and mean.

"How did *you* get here?" she asked. And I knew she was really, really mad.

"We went a different way," I said.

"There isn't a different way!" Zoe

shouted. "There isn't! There's just one way. And it had a traffic jam!"

"There must be," Miss Amy said. "Because look—Ella's here. Now sit down, Zoe, and please stop shouting."

Zoe sat down, but she still looked grumpy. She banged her bag on the table.

I didn't say anything else. I just kept coloring. I thought about Mom and the flying car. I thought about being invisible and the jelly legs and the bull and the rocket blasters. I thought about me and Mom saving everyone from the traffic jam, and what Dad would say when he saw the car. I drew it all in my book. And I stroked my special shiny sticker and smiled.

Fairy Spell #2

SPAGHETTERIDOO!

The Great Pasta Playdate

My best friends, Tom and Lenka, were coming to my house on Saturday, and I was so excited! At school on Friday, we made a plan for the playdate. Lenka was bringing her puppet theater, and we were going to put on a show. The story was about a princess and a prince and a scary dragon, because those are the puppets Lenka has.

Tom said he would be the scary dragon. But Lenka wanted to be the scary dragon too, and so did I. We all started to get frustrated— until Lenka said, "Why don't we take turns being the scary dragon?"

Lenka is good at fixing arguments.

Then Zoe came past. She tossed her head

and said, "Your stupid playdate sounds really boring."

Zoe always says mean things like that, which is why she is my Not-Best Friend. I ignored her, because Mom says it is always best to ignore mean people. But then Zoe added, "Ella's house is really weird. Her whole *family* is weird." And she wrinkled her nose as though she could smell something bad.

I got really mad then. "My house is *not* weird!"

"Yes it is. It's weird and strange," Zoe said.

Then Tom stepped in. "*You're* weird and strange, Zoe."

Lenka and I giggled, and Tom started laughing too. Zoe's eyes went very small and angry. "I'm telling Miss Amy on you!" she screamed.

Then she ran off, but I knew she wouldn't tell Miss Amy, because then we would tell her who started it.

Once we stopped giggling, Tom turned to me. "Are we still having spaghetti at your house this weekend, Ella?"

"Of course!"

I had told Mom lots of times that Tom and Lenka's favorite food was spaghetti, and she had promised to make it. I love spaghetti too. (Except not when it has cheese on it.)

"Yum!" Tom said. "I'm going to bring my special spaghetti fork. It has a battery and it twirls around and around and it's awesome."

I couldn't wait to see Tom's spaghetti fork and I couldn't wait to put on the puppet show. It was going to be the best play-date ever!

On Saturday I woke up really early and gazed at my unicorn poster for a while. I love my unicorn poster. Then I got up and looked around the house. It didn't look strange or weird—but it did look messy. So I decided to do something about it.

"Come on, Wardrobe!" I said. "We're going to clean up."

Wardrobe is my magic pet wardrobe. I'm training it to do what I say. It's a bit like having a dog, except Wardrobe is more wooden than a dog and doesn't say "Woof."

Wardrobe followed me around the house on its little legs. I picked up books, toys and odd socks off the floor and threw them into Wardrobe. Wardrobe helped by swinging open its doors to catch things and shuffling things along with its feet.

Just when everything was tidied up, Mom came out of her bedroom holding my little brother, Ollie. She said, "Good morning, Ella! Good morning, Wardrobe!" And Wardrobe made a loud noise: Burrrp.

"Wardrobe! That's rude!"

"Wardrobe sounds full to me," Mom said. "I've bought some delicious sausages for your playdate, Ella. We can make mashed potatoes too."

I stared at Mom in shock. I said, "But what about the spaghetti?"

Mom stared back, then hit her forehead.

"Spaghetti!" she said. "I forgot. Well, don't worry, Ella. I'm sure we've got spaghetti."

But when Mom emptied the spaghetti packet into a pot, there was only one lonely strand. It went *ping!* as it landed. Then it broke in two.

"Oh no," Mom said. "I think we need some magic."

"Or a trip to the store?" I suggested, because sometimes Mom's magic doesn't work.

"Nonsense!" she said. "A spell will be much quicker."

She stamped her feet three times, clapped her hands, wiggled her bottom and said, "Marshmallow," . . . and POOF! She was a fairy, with glittery wings and a crown.

"We need some drinks too," she said. "What would you like?"

"Tom likes orange juice," I said.

"Easy-peasy," Mom said. She pressed a code on her Computawand—*bleep-bleep-bloop*—and said, "Orangeridoo!"

At once her face and arms turned orange.

"Mom!" I said. "You've gone orange!" Then I looked at *my* arms. "So have I!"

"Weezi-weezi-weezi!" said Ollie, who had turned bright orange too.

"Oops," Mom said, peering at her Computawand. "I don't know how *that* happened."

Just then Dad came in. His face was orange as well.

"I'm orange!" he said. "I look like a carrot!"

"Never mind," Mom said. She pressed another code—*bleep-bleep-bloop*—and said, **"Normeridoo!"** At once our skin went back to normal.

"Phew," Dad said. "Maybe that's enough magic for today."

"No!" Mom said. "I need to make

spaghetti. I promised Ella. Don't worry—spaghetti is a very easy spell."

She pointed her Computawand at the saucepot, pressed a code—*bleep-bleep-bloop*—and said, "Spaghetteridoo!"

All at once spaghetti started filling up the pan. But it wasn't dried spaghetti—it was cooked spaghetti, all soft and floppy. It quickly filled the pot, spilled over the top and began piling up on the floor.

"*What happened?*" Dad asked.

"Mom!" I said. "That's too much spaghetti! We only need three platefuls!"

"It's cold," said Dad, touching a strand. "Cold spaghetti. Oh dear."

"Weezi-weezi-weezi!" Ollie yelled

joyfully. He grabbed some spaghetti off the floor and piled it on his head.

"Oops," Mom said, peering at the spaghetti. "I don't know how *that* happened."

She quickly pressed a code on her Computawand, but it didn't go *bleep-bleep-bloop* like it normally does. It just went *bleep-bleep*.

She tried again—but it went *bleep-bleep* again.

"Oh no! The button is stuck!" said Mom. She jabbed at the button again. "Come on, you silly Computawand!"

"Hurry!" Dad said.

Spaghetti kept pouring out of the pot. By now there was spaghetti all over the kitchen floor, and in the hall too. It was like a big, thick spaghetti carpet. Ollie was rolling around in it, laughing and kicking.

Suddenly I remembered something I had read in one of Mom's fairy magazines.

"Mom!" I said. "You can use honey if a button on your Computawand gets stuck."

"Honey!" Mom said. "Of course. Well done, Ella."

She grabbed some honey from the cupboard and spooned a tiny bit onto the stuck button. At last it worked. She pressed the code—*bleep-bleep-bloop*—and shouted, "Stoperidoo!"

The spaghetti stopped pouring out of the pot and we all looked at each other.

"Well, at least it's stopped," Mom said.

"Yes," Dad said. "But I've never seen so much spaghetti in my life!"

There was spaghetti *every-where*. It was on the counter and the floor—some was even hanging from the lampshade.

"What should we do with it?" I said. "We can't eat it. Ollie has rolled and drooled all over it."

Mom looked at her Computawand. "I could do another spell," she said.

"Or I could get the wheelbarrow," Dad said.

"Yes," Mom said. "Maybe that's a better idea. Toffee apple!" And at once she was a normal mom again.

Dad got his wheelbarrow and we carted all the spaghetti into the backyard. It took lots of trips back and forth. We made a pile and covered it with leaves. Dad said that when it dried out, we could have a bonfire.

At last we went inside, puffing—and the doorbell rang. It was Lenka and her mom, holding the puppet theater.

"Are we too early?" Lenka's mom asked.

"No!" Mom said. "Perfect timing! Come in."

Lenka and her mom came in and showed

us the puppet theater, and Mom made some coffee.

Suddenly Lenka's mom gasped. "Goodness!" she said. "What an amazing costume!"

Mom and Dad and I turned around, and we gasped too. Ollie had come into the kitchen *covered* in spaghetti. I realized what had happened—

he had gone into the backyard and rolled
in the spaghetti pile. And there he was, all
wrapped up in spaghetti like a big round
meatball.

Lenka and her mom looked so surprised
that I felt worried. Lenka would think my
house was really strange and weird.

"Is that real spaghetti?" she asked, and her mom laughed.

"Of course it's not real spaghetti, Lenka. No one has that much spaghetti!"

"Actually, I think Ollie's diaper needs changing," Dad said quickly. "I'll do it." He picked him up and took him upstairs.

Then the doorbell rang again, and it was Tom.

While our moms all drank coffee, Tom, Lenka and I set up the puppet theater in the hall, next to Wardrobe, which had been cleaning up downstairs. We were just getting the puppets out when there was a loud noise: Burrrp.

Lenka and Tom
looked shocked.

"Ella," Tom said.
"Did that wardrobe
just . . . burp?"

"How could a wardrobe burp?" I asked. I tried to laugh—but I felt worried again.

"Your house isn't like anyone else's, Ella," Lenka said. "It's really cool."

"Yeah," Tom agreed. "It's cool."

Happiness whooshed through me. I knew our house was different from other people's—and now I felt proud of it.

Then Dad came downstairs holding Ollie. All the spaghetti was gone. He winked at me and said, "I'm going out to buy some more spaghetti. Who wants ice cream?"

Tom and Lenka shouted, "Yay!"

That afternoon, after Tom and Lenka went home, I sat in the kitchen drawing pictures of everything we'd done. I drew the puppets and Tom's twirling spaghetti fork. Then I drew our kitchen covered in spaghetti and I started to laugh. I showed my picture to Mom, and she laughed too.

I said, "Our house isn't like anyone else's, is it?" and she said, "No, Ella, it certainly isn't. And we are not like anyone else."

I drew a picture of Wardrobe and colored it in. Then I said, "Zoe thinks we're strange and weird. But Tom and Lenka think we're cool."

Mom kissed me on the head and said, "What do you think we are?"

I thought for a bit, and then I said, "I think we're cool."

"I think we're cool too," said Mom. "I think we're *super*-cool."

"We're super-super-*super*-cool," I said. And I looked up at her and smiled.

Fairy Spell #3

TWIRLERIDOO!

Sheep Don't Dance, Do They?

One day I was watching Mom having her magic lesson with Fenella on FairyTube. She was learning about the Rainbow Effect.

The Rainbow Effect is very powerful and mysterious. When there is a rainbow in the sky, fairies have to be careful because their spells are extra strong and very hard to control.

That's why there's a Rainbow App on every Computawand. The app tells you when a rainbow is coming. All fairies have them except Granny. She doesn't like apps or Computawands. She says, "Just look at the sky, dear."

When Mom finished her lesson, I turned to her. "I wish *I* could have magic lessons."

Mom smiled. "You can't have magic lessons yet, Ella. But guess what. You're going to start dancing lessons!"

"Yay!" I said, excited. "Dancing!" I started to dance around the room, whirling my arms.

"Weezi-weezi-weezi!" Ollie shouted. He whirled his arms too, and knocked his breadsticks all over the floor.

I couldn't wait for dancing lessons. I went shopping with Mom and we bought pink ballet shoes. I wanted to buy a pink tutu with a frilly skirt, but we were in a hurry, so Mom said maybe another time.

When we arrived for the first lesson, there

were lots of children there. One of them was Zoe, my Not-Best Friend from next door.

"Oh look," Mom said. "Zoe does dancing too. That's good, isn't it?"

Sometimes Mom doesn't understand about Zoe. It wasn't good—it was bad, because Zoe is always mean to me. But luckily she didn't see me. She was in the front row, doing very high jumps with pointy toes.

I tried to copy her—but I fell over.

"Never mind!" Mom said. "It's never easy when you start, Ella. But keep trying. I know you can do it. Have fun!"

Then Zoe saw me. She came over and said in her mean voice, "Oh, Ella, *you're* here.

I'm really good at dancing. I've been coming here forever. I bet you're really bad."

"I bet I'm *not*," I said.

I decided to try my best at dancing. I watched the teacher, Miss Evans, demonstrate. We raised our arms. We did a special jump called a cat jump. I said, "Meow!" when I jumped, because it made me feel like a cat.

At the end of the lesson Miss Evans said, "We have a special treat today. Zoe's cousin Sally is here. Sally is a real grown-up ballerina, and she is going to show us her dancing."

Sally was wearing a lovely swishy skirt. She told us how she practiced dancing every day. Then she danced on her tiptoes. She did twirls, around and around. We all clapped and cheered. I wanted to do a twirl so, *so* badly, but I didn't know how.

On our way out we all thanked Sally for showing us her dancing.

"I wish I could do a twirl," I said.

"I'm sure you will one day!" Sally said. "Keep trying!"

But Zoe was standing nearby. She came close so no one could hear, then said, "*You'll* never do a twirl, Ella. You can't even point your toes the right way. You're bad at dancing." And she laughed her horrible laugh.

* * *

That weekend it was very sunny. Mom, Ollie and I went for a picnic with Aunty Jo. We drove out into the countryside and sat on some grass. All the fields around us had animals in them. One had sheep, one had pigs and one had two horses. I gave some carrots to the horses over the fence. I tried to give a carrot to a sheep, but it ran away.

"Have a sandwich, Ella," Mom shouted, and I hurried back to the picnic blanket. But just as I took a bite, it started raining.

"Oh no!" I said. "What about our picnic?"

"Don't worry!" Aunty Jo said. "Fairy to the rescue!"

She looked around to check that no one

could see us. Then she stamped her feet three times, clapped her hands, wiggled her bottom and said, "Sherbet lemon," . . . and POOF! She was a fairy with shining wings and a beautiful diamond crown.

She held out her Computawand, pressed a code—*bleep-bleep-bloop*—and shouted, "Umbrelleridoo!"

Suddenly a great big floating umbrella appeared above us. It had green and white stripes and was so enormous it kept the rain off us all. Aunty Jo is very good at magic.

While we ate our picnic, I told Aunty Jo all about my dancing lessons. I even got my

bag out of the car and showed her my pink ballet shoes. I told her how much I wanted to do a twirl. Then Aunty Jo turned to me. "You need the Twirleridoo spell!"

At once I felt excited. A Twirleridoo spell sounded really cool!

But Mom did not look happy. "Jo, Ella needs to learn dancing through hard work, not through magic."

"Oh, I know," Aunty Jo said. "Of course. Hard work and all that. But why don't I just *show* Ella the Twirleridoo spell? Look, the rain has stopped."

Aunty Jo Fairy walked into the middle of the field, pointed her Computawand at

herself, pressed a code—*bleep-bleep-bloop*—
and shouted, "Twirleridoo!"

I gasped, because ballet shoes appeared
on Aunty Jo's feet, and she started whizzing
around on one leg. She was much faster than
Sally the ballerina. Every time she slowed
down she shouted, "Twirleridoo!" and started
twirling again.

I clapped and cried, "Amazing!" I wanted
to ask if I could do it too, but I knew Mom
would say no.

Just then I glanced up at the sky. It was blue
again. The sun was out and there was a rainbow. At first I thought, *A rainbow—yay!* Then
I remembered about the Rainbow Effect.

"Mom!" I said quickly. "Watch out! There's a rainbow!"

"A *rainbow*?" Mom looked up. "My Rainbow App said it would be tomorrow. Jo!" she called. "Watch out! Rainbow!"

"Aunty Jo!" I shouted. "Rainbow!"

But Aunty Jo couldn't hear either of us. She was saying, "Twirleridoo!" and whizzing around.

Mom ran toward
Aunty Jo, pointing at
the sky and yelling,
"Jo! RAINBOW!"

At last Aunty Jo heard. She
stopped saying "Twirleridoo"
and slowed down. "It's fine,"
she panted. "No harm done.
Everything's fine, everything's
normal."

But everything wasn't fine and everything wasn't normal.

"Look!" I gasped. *"Look!"*

I was staring at the sheep in the nearest field. They were all twirling around on one foot, just like Aunty Jo. They were wearing purple ballet shoes and saying "Baaa!" while they twirled, as though they didn't understand what was going on.

"Dancing *sheep?*" Mom asked when she saw them. "Jo, what have you *done?*"

"It's not my fault!" Aunty Jo said. "It's the Rainbow Effect."

"Look, dancing pigs!" I said, pointing to the next field. The pigs were twirling too, in little piggy ballet shoes, only theirs were blue.

"Weezi-weezi-weezi!" said Ollie, and he pointed at the horses. They were both

twirling and tossing their manes. All the animals were dancing in different-colored ballet

shoes. Even the squirrels in the tree were twirling on the branches and looking very surprised.

I couldn't stop laughing, but Mom looked worried.

"The Rainbow Effect is very special and powerful," she said. "It can't be undone with a spell. We'll just have to wait for it to wear off."

Just then, a farmer in an old brown jacket came walking across the grass.

"Oh no!" said Mom. "I hope he doesn't notice anything wrong."

But as soon as the farmer looked into the first field, he stopped. "What's happened to my sheep?" he demanded. "They look like whirligigs!" Then he saw the pigs. "What's happened to my pigs?" he gasped. "They're dancing too! Pigs aren't supposed to dance!"

"Er . . . maybe they got bored?" Aunty Jo said.

Then the farmer saw the horses, and I thought he was going to fall over in shock. One of the horses was holding the other

horse by its hooves, and they were both twirling around.

"Dapple!" the farmer shouted. "Beauty! What do you think you're doing? You're not blooming ballerinas—you're *horses*."

"I think they're stopping," said Mom after a moment, and it was true.

Gradually all the ballet shoes disappeared. The sheep started eating grass again, like

normal sheep. The pigs

started rooting around in

the mud. The two horses trotted off.

I was sad—I had loved watching the dancing animals.

"Awayeridoo!" Aunty Jo shouted, pointing
her Computawand at the floating umbrella,
and it disappeared.

The farmer's mouth fell open. "What's
going on?" he said. "Are you aliens?"

"No," said Aunty Jo Fairy. "We're fairies."

"Aunty Jo Fairy!" I said, shocked. "You
told him!"

"Yes," she said, winking at me. "But
he won't remember." Then she said,

"Blueberry pie!" and at once she was just Aunty Jo again.

Then Mom took some Fairy Dust out of her bag and threw it over the farmer. For about ten seconds he was completely still, as if he had gone to sleep.

"Go!" Mom said, and he woke up.

He smiled politely at us all. "Hello," he said. "Are you having a nice picnic? Did you see that lovely rainbow?"

"Oh yes," said Mom. "We certainly did."

When I arrived at my next dancing lesson, I kept thinking about the twirling sheep. I decided I would try to twirl exactly like them.

As I put on my ballet shoes, I noticed that they looked strange. They were gleaming as if a rainbow was shining on them. I didn't understand why, but I put them on and went into the class.

I stepped onto one foot and started to turn—and just for fun I said, very quietly, "Twirleridoo!"

To my surprise I did a perfect twirl! Then another one!

I couldn't understand how I was twirling. Then I looked down at my shiny rainbow shoes again and realized that it was the Rainbow Effect! There was some left in my shoes!

"Look at Ella!" a boy named Callum cried. "She's really good!"

I twirled around again and again. My legs were just doing it by themselves!

I didn't know how, but they were! I could

see Zoe staring furiously at me, but I didn't care. I felt like a real ballerina.

"How come you can do that, Ella?" she shouted. "You're only a beginner!"

I hoped my shoes would stay magic forever, but already the rainbow light was fading. I did one last twirl—and then it was gone. The magic was over. The next time I stepped onto one foot, it didn't know how to twirl anymore. It felt all heavy and strange.

"Do it again!" Callum said.

"I can't," I said.

Just then Miss Evans came in. Everyone rushed up and told her how I had been twirling.

"Show me, Ella," she said with a smile.

But I said, "I've forgotten how."

"Never mind," she said kindly. "I'm sure you'll learn again."

"I'm sure she won't," Zoe said, looking at me with her small, angry eyes. "Anyway, her twirls weren't that good."

"Zoe," Miss Evans said. "That is not polite."

The whole room was silent, and Zoe turned pink.

"In this class," Miss Evans started, "we say *kind* things to our classmates."

Then we started our lesson and I tried my hardest. We didn't do twirls, but we did snowflakes. I tried to be a very light snowflake—except I was too busy looking at Miss Evans and crashed into Callum by mistake. He said, "Snow*flake*! Not snow*storm*!" and we all laughed.

While we were getting ready to go home,
Zoe stayed in the middle of the room doing
twirls. I remembered what Miss Evans had
told us about saying kind things. Zoe isn't

a nice person, but she is still good at twirls. So I went up to her and said, "You twirl really well, Zoe! You're just as good as a sheep."

As soon as I said it, I realized I shouldn't have said "sheep." Zoe stared at me with her tiny, furious eyes. She shouted, "A *sheep*? Miss Evans, Ella called me a sheep!"

Everyone started to laugh.

"I meant it in a *good* way!" I said. "I was being nice!" But I could tell that Zoe didn't believe me.

"Ella called me a sheep!" she wailed, and she started crying loudly. (Though I think she was pretending.)

"Ella," Miss Evans said, coming over. "Why did you call Zoe a sheep? I'm very disappointed."

I felt as if I might cry myself. I didn't want Miss Evans to be disappointed, but I didn't know how to reply. Then, suddenly, I heard Mom's voice saying, "I can explain!"

"Really?" Miss Evans asked.

"Oh yes," said Mom. "Zoe, Ella didn't mean to offend you. The truth is . . . we once saw a whole field of wonderful, graceful dancing sheep."

I gazed at her, astonished. Was she going to tell everyone about Twirleridoo and being a fairy?

But then Mom added, "In a book. Of course." And she winked at me.

In the car on the way home, I told Mom about my twirls and took my ballet shoes out of my bag. I wanted to see if there were any shiny bits of the Rainbow Effect left in them, even a tiny speck. But they were just normal pink ballet shoes.

"I wish I could still twirl," I said. "I wish I still had the Rainbow Effect on my shoes. When I'm grown up I'll do the Twirleridoo spell every day."

"I'm sure you will," said Mom, nodding. She drove on for a bit, then said, "But that's a long time to wait. What about for now?"

I thought about trying to twirl.

I thought about Sally whizzing around.

I thought about how she practiced dancing every day. And I decided I wanted to be like her.

"For now," I said, "I'll practice twirling every day until I can do it."

"Good idea, Ella," said Mom. "That's my girl." And she looked over at me, and we both smiled.

Fairy Spell #4

GLITCHERIDOO!

A Unicorn in the Kitchen

One day I was in the kitchen reading Mom's Spell Book. It was written long ago by the Old, Old Fairies. Every fairy has one, even though lots of them use their Fairy Apps now. I was reading about Bad Magic. If you try to use magic to be lazy or mean or cruel, it is called Bad Magic and it won't turn out well.

Mom was making a cup of coffee.

"Mom," I said. "When I'm a grown-up fairy, I'll never use Bad Magic."

"Good girl, Ella," she said, smiling at me.

Then Aunty Jo arrived. She was very excited. She said, "Have you heard about the super-cool new Fairy App? It's called Auto-Spell! Let's all watch the ad!"

Aunty Jo loves buying apps for her Computawand. Mom says most of them are a waste of money, as they always glitch. (That means they get stuck or go wrong.) But even so, she opened FairyTube on her laptop and we all watched the ad for Auto-Spell. A fairy was holding her Computawand while her bicycle mended itself. She smiled and said, *"Auto-Spell is the first Fairy App that can read your mind. It casts the spell you need even before you know you need it! Buy Auto-Spell now!"*

"This will make magic so easy," Aunty Jo said. "I'm going to buy it."

Mom stared at the screen for a bit. Then she said, "I'm going to buy it too."

I was so excited. We were going to have a super-cool new app!

When Auto-Spell arrived, it looked like a tiny gold coin. It wasn't like a normal app that you can just buy from the app store. Mom fitted it into a special slot in her Computawand. She screwed the panel shut and turned it on. Then she stamped her feet three times, clapped her hands, wiggled her bottom and said, "Marshmallow," . . . and POOF! She was a fairy.

Meanwhile, I was looking at the instruction booklet. It had lots of pictures of fairies holding cups of tea and watching lawn mowers working. The writing said:

Auto-Spell

Welcome to Auto-Spell! Simply relax and think your normal thoughts. Auto-Spell will read your mind and cast all the spells you wish for.

Auto-Spell

1.   2.   3.

I said, "Mom, should I read the instructions aloud?"

But Mom said, "Don't worry, Ella. I expect I can work it out as I go."

Mom never reads instruction booklets, but I like looking at them and coloring the pictures.

Mom came over to the kitchen table and the chair pulled itself out.

"Thank you, Auto-Spell!" she said, sitting down. Then the teapot lifted itself up and poured her some tea. Mom looked pleased.

"Isn't this wonderful?" she said to Dad. "Tea was exactly what I wanted."

Then the cornflakes box rose into the air and poured me a big bowl of cornflakes.

"Thank you, Mom!" I said. "Thank you, Auto-Spell!"

I wanted a nice big breakfast because I was going to the park with Tom and Lenka. Tom's dad was going to teach us some soccer skills.

At that moment Aunty Jo came in through the back door. She was breathing hard, as though she had been running.

"Have you got the Auto-Spell app?" she asked. "Is it any good? Mine hasn't arrived yet."

"Yes!" Mom said. "It's amazing! It's reading my mind. It's doing everything I want."

Just then a big plate of pancakes covered in chocolate sauce and marshmallows landed on the table.

"Mmm!" I said. "Thank you, Mom! Thank you, Auto-Spell!"

Mom looked puzzled. "I didn't want pancakes," she said, just as a huge strawberry milk shake with a straw appeared in front of me.

"Strawberry is my favorite!" I said. "And I love straws!"

Mom stared at me. "Ella, did you imagine me having a cup of tea just now?"

"Yes," I said. "You always have a cup of tea for breakfast, Mom. And toast."

As I said the word "toast," a toast rack

floated down toward Mom. It was full of toast.

Mom gasped in horror. "I think Auto-Spell is reading the wrong mind!" she said. "It has tuned into Ella's mind instead of mine!"

"Tragic," Aunty Jo said, shaking her head. "Didn't you read the instruction booklet? I *always* do."

"Ella, you must stop thinking of things," Dad

said as Mom grabbed the instructions. "Do you understand? Don't think about *anything.*"

"Okay, Dad," I said. "I'll try."

But it's hard not to think about anything. Just then there was a neighing sound from the hall. A unicorn was standing at the kitchen door, looking in at us. It had a fluffy white mane, and its horn was glittering in the sunlight.

"Ella, did you wish for a unicorn?" asked Mom.

"I always wish for a unicorn," I said. "All the time."

The unicorn came into the kitchen and I put my arms around it. It was so soft and gentle that I kissed it. I felt so happy. I had a real unicorn!

Then a chocolate fountain appeared in the middle of the kitchen.

"Ella!" Aunty Jo exclaimed. "Stop thinking!"

I tried my hardest not to think about anything—but I couldn't. Soon there were lots of kittens all over the kitchen, mewing and licking their paws. There was a merry-go-round in the backyard, and I had a lollipop in my hand.

Ollie was sitting in his high chair

watching the kittens. He banged his spoon on his tray and said, "Weezi-weezi-weezi!"

I thought, *I wish Ollie could talk already,* just like I always do.

Then Ollie said, "Wow! I can talk now. Hello, Ella. You're an awesome big sister."

I clapped my hand over my mouth. I had made Ollie talk!

"Enough!" Dad said, looking shocked. "We have to stop this *now*!"

"I'm trying to remove the app," Mom said, "but I can't get it out!" She was trying to open the panel on her Computawand with a screwdriver, but it seemed to be stuck.

Suddenly Aunty Jo screamed. A huge, scary eye was looking in at us through the kitchen window.

"Ella!" Aunty Jo said. "Don't wish for a dinosaur!"

"I didn't!" I said.

"Dinosaur!" Ollie cried joyfully. "I love dinosaurs!" He waved his hands at the dinosaur, and I gasped.

"Mom! I think the app is reading *Ollie's* mind now!"

At that moment there was a roaring sound, and a little red steam train came puffing into the kitchen.

"Ella, I think you're right!" Dad said.

"I'm a train driver," Ollie said. "That's my train. *Choo choo!*"

But then the train turned into a big red snake and we all screamed.

"Who wished for a snake?" Dad asked.

"Nobody!" I said.

Snow started falling from the ceiling, and thunder rumbled in the sky. The snake hissed. The dinosaur batted the window with its head and roared angrily at us, and I shivered in fright.

"The app is glitching!" Aunty Jo exclaimed.

"Everything's so scary!" Ollie screamed.
"I don't understand! I want my teddy bear!"
Then he started crying. "Waaaah!"

Mom was still struggling with her

Computawand. "Quick," she said to Aunty Jo. "We need the Glitcheridoo spell!"

Aunty Jo stamped her feet three times, clapped her hands, wiggled her bottom and said, "Sherbet lemon." At once she was a fairy, with big, strong, shiny wings. She pressed a code—*bleep-bleep-bloop*—then pointed her Computawand at the snake and shouted, "Glitcheridoo!" It disappeared.

Then she made the dinosaur disappear.

"Thank goodness!" said Dad.

But then a great big tentacle came through the kitchen door. There was an octopus in the hall! It was huge and slimy, and it was coming toward us!

"The app is still glitching!" Aunty Jo cried. "Glitcheridoo!"

She quickly made the octopus

disappear, but the next minute a sea lion appeared in the sink. The floor started swaying back and forth, and the sky turned pink.

"Hurry!" Aunty Jo said to Mom. "Everything is very strange!"

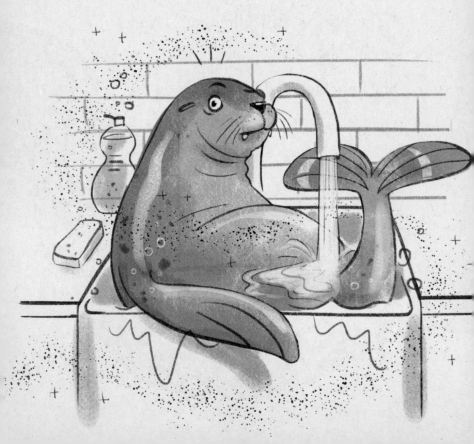

At last Mom got the panel on her Computawand open and pulled out the gold coin.

There was a sort of **crash!** and a flash of light—then everything was quiet. All the strange things had disappeared. The world was back to normal. We were all breathing hard, looking at each other.

"Well!" Mom said at last. "I didn't expect that!"

I looked at the app in her hand. It was such a tiny gold coin, but it had created so much trouble.

Suddenly I realized what had happened.

"I think the app is Bad Magic. It's using magic to be lazy. That's why it went wrong."

Aunty Jo Fairy looked very surprised.

"Ella, how do you know about Bad Magic?" she asked. "That's very grown up."

"I read about it in Mom's Spell Book," I told her.

"Well, I think you're right," said Aunty Jo Fairy. "Auto-Spell is Bad Magic. I'll send my app back."

"I'm sending mine back too," Mom said. "I'm going to complain."

"Weezi-weezi-weezi!" Ollie said, banging his spoon. I was so glad he was back to normal that I went to give him a great big hug.

The only thing I was sad about was my unicorn. I had loved it so much, and now it was gone.

"Can I have a unicorn one day?" I asked. "A real unicorn?"

"Maybe," Mom said. "When you're a grown-up fairy."

I decided that the minute I was a grown-up fairy I would have a unicorn. And ten kittens. And ice cream every day.

Two weeks later, Mom came into the kitchen holding her laptop. She said, "Look at this, Ella."

She was watching news on FairyTube. A fairy was looking very serious as she said, *"The new Auto-Spell app has been banned. It is Bad Magic, and it has caused a lot of trouble. If you've bought the Auto-Spell app, please send it back to the Fairy Store, and you will get your money back."*

Mom pressed PAUSE. "You were right, Ella. Well done!" Then she said, "Maybe you will invent a Fairy App one day. A *good* Fairy App."

I thought about the Fairy App I would invent one day. It would be very useful and clever. Maybe it would give food to hungry people. Or maybe it would stop people from having accidents.

Then I remembered the pink sky and the thunder and the dinosaur's scary eye. I looked at Mom, and I said, "If I invent a Fairy App, it will definitely not glitch. *Ever.*"

Mom laughed and said, "Certainly not! No glitches for Ella!"

"Weezi-weezi-weezi!" said Ollie, as if he was agreeing.

"That's right, Ollie," I said. "No glitches for me." And I looked up at Mom and smiled.

FAMILY ACTIVITY GUIDE— FOR MORE FAIRY FUN!

BAGSERIDOO!

Design your own fairy handbag!

What do you think a fairy would keep in her handbag? Write a list here! There are a couple of ideas to start you off.

Computawand

Fairy Dust

RAINBOWERIDOO!

Make your own rainbow appear with this fun activity—and don't forget to add glitter to make it look extra special!

✳ Make sure you ask a grown-up to help you cut it out.

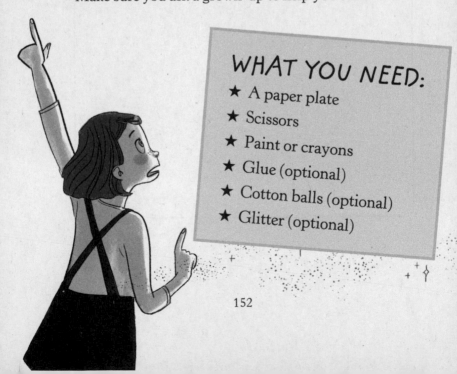

WHAT YOU NEED:
- ★ A paper plate
- ★ Scissors
- ★ Paint or crayons
- ★ Glue (optional)
- ★ Cotton balls (optional)
- ★ Glitter (optional)

WHAT TO DO:

1 With a grown-up's help, cut the paper plate in half. Next, cut out a semicircle from the middle of the plate, to get a rainbow shape.

2 Use your paint or crayons to color stripes for your rainbow. Follow the curve of the plate. You can start from the top or bottom curve. Ask a grown-up to draw lines to follow, if that makes it easier.

3 The colors of a rainbow are (starting from the top): red, orange, yellow, green, blue, purple and violet (light purple). But don't worry if you don't have all these colors. A magical rainbow can have any colors you like, in any order!

4 If you like, you can glue cotton balls to the bottom of your rainbow, for the clouds.

5 Add glitter to your rainbow to show that it's full of rainbow magic! Next time you see a rainbow in the sky, watch out for anything unusual on your street or in your town. It might be a sign that rainbow magic is really happening. . . .

FINDERIDOO!

Can you spot these words
in the word search?

(Answers on page 159.)

APP

GLITCH

RAINBOW

SPAGHETTI

SPARKLE

SPELL BOOK

UMBRELLA

UNICORN

M	Y	D	I	F	C	Z	F	J	A	C	R
I	U	X	K	V	L	T	P	I	L	C	T
I	T	T	E	H	G	A	P	S	L	X	P
K	W	U	W	P	L	S	F	Y	E	C	W
E	O	F	N	F	I	W	L	W	R	O	W
J	W	O	A	I	T	Y	X	P	ß	L	X
K	K	P	ß	Y	C	V	N	N	M	Z	T
R	P	O	P	L	H	O	I	Y	U	H	J
K	D	F	O	I	L	A	R	C	I	J	L
G	S	V	Q	K	R	E	W	N	T	O	L
C	V	H	Q	O	N	C	P	T	V	A	C
S	P	A	R	K	L	E	S	S	H	W	ß

WISHERIDOO!

If you had the Auto-Spell app, what would you wish for? A unicorn, like Ella—or something else? Draw your wishes here!

ANSWERS

FINDERIDOO!

Fairy Mom and Me

illustrated by
Marta Kissi

New York Times bestselling author
SOPHIE KINSELLA

"Inventive and charming. Definitely deserving
of a place on the nightstand." —Booklist

Fairy In Waiting

illustrated by
Marta Kissi

New York Times bestselling author

SOPHIE KINSELLA

"Messages about the virtues of patience and not taking shortcuts are handled with a light touch—most readers will be content to laugh over the fairy magic hijinks." —Publishers Weekly

Fairy Mermaid Magic
coming soon

"Fun stuff for the fairy-focused."
—Kirkus Reviews

More fairy fun!